With much love to my dear friends Craig and Martene –
and especially Elsie, who has a lifetime of love ahead of her.
C.S.

With all my love to my own messy monsters, Johnny and Anna!
B.C.

First published in 2012 by Scholastic Children's Books
This edition published in 2013
Euston House, 24 Eversholt Street
London NW1 1DB
a division of Scholastic Ltd
www.scholastic.co.uk
London ~ New York ~ Toronto ~ Sydney ~ Auckland
Mexico City ~ New Delhi ~ Hong Kong

Text copyright © 2012 Chae Strathie
Illustrations copyright © 2012 Ben Cort

PB ISBN 978 1407 10801 8

Printed in Singapore

5 7 9 10 8 6 4

The moral rights of Chae Strathie and Ben Cort have been asserted.

Papers used by Scholastic Children's Books are made from wood grown in sustainable forests.

Jumblebum

Written by Chae Strathie
Illustrated by Ben Cort

SCHOLASTIC

This is the story of Johnny McNess,
Whose room was an eye-popping,
tum-churning MESS.

There was gunk on the carpet
and junk on the bed,
And underpants draped
over Bob the dog's head!

There were beans in his trainers
and jam on his toys,
And strange creepy-crawlies
that made an odd noise.

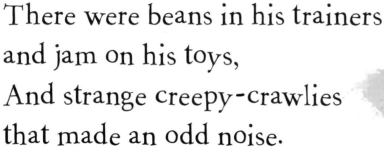

The curtains were crumpled
and covered in scribbles,
And dripping with ketchup
and yogurty dribbles.

And if all that awfulness wasn't enough,
His sock drawer was bursting with mountains of fluff.

"Careful," warned Mum,
growing faint with the pong,
Holding her nose
as the smell was so strong.

"All of this stuff
lying crinkled and creased
Is sure to attract the

JUMBLEBUM
BEAST!"

"I can't see what's wrong,"
Johnny said with a smile.
"I think that my room
has its own special style."

But later that night, as he snoozled and snored,
Something was stirring down there on the floor.

That something was smelly,
that something was big,

That something went "snuffle"
and "snort" like a pig.

For there in the corner, enjoying a feast,
Was the horribly slobbery

JUMBLEBUM BEAST!

Its body was made
out of wrinkled-up clothes,

All grubby and gross
from its head to its toes.

Its hot stinky breath
reeked of smelly old shoes,

And out of its mouth
leaked a luminous OOZE.

The beast made a sound like a rusty trombone,
And Johnny woke up with a bleary-eyed groan.

"HARRUMPH! HARROO!"
the Jumblebum howled.
Then, spotting Johnny,
it let out a growl...

"I've had quite enough of eating these clothes,

I think I might SNACK ON A LITTLE PINK NOSE.

I bet KIDS TASTE BETTER than T-shirts and pants And mouldy green hamburgers covered in ants."

The beast licked his lips,
then let out a roar,
But Johnny was fast
and he dashed for the door.

He ran down the hall
with the thing close behind.
But where could he go
that was tricky to find?

The kitchen was perfect!
A shadowy room –
He wouldn't be seen
tucked away in the gloom.

But the monster thumped in
and it sniffled the air...
Peered under the table...
and guess who was there?

"HARRUMPH! HARROO!" cried the vile Jumblebum.
"You're about to end up in my fat Jumble tum!"

But Johnny was smarter
than most other snacks,
And had clever ways
to avoid such attacks.

The creature leaped forward,
its mouth open wide,
But Johnny was quick
and he stepped to one side.

And right in the spot
where he'd only just been,
Was the thing
that would save him…

THE
WASHING
MACHINE!

The monster plunged in from its head to its feet,
And spluttered with rage,
"That's not fair – you're a cheat!"

It let out a gurgle as Mum sprinted in
And reached for the button marked...

"EXTRA FAST SPIN!"

Since then Johnny's managed
to pull off a feat:
That bedroom of his
is now lovely and neat.

And you would be wise to listen to Mum –
Just in case that wasn't the last

JUMBLEBUM!